Peppa Pig

Rainy Day

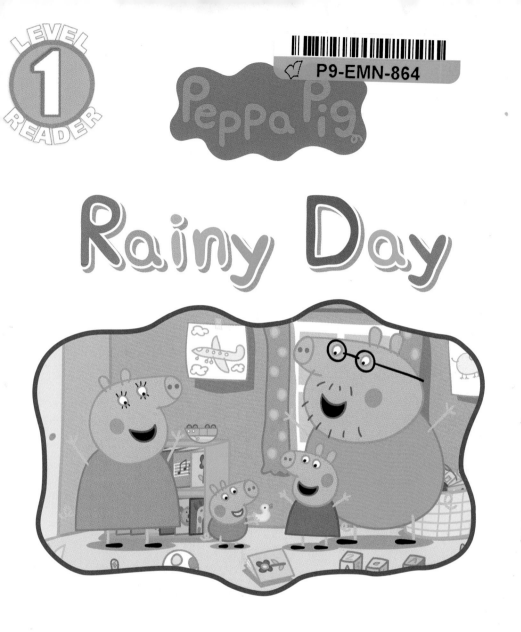

Adapted by Katie Cicatelli-Kuc

SCHOLASTIC INC.

ISBN 978-1-338-85959-1

10 9 8 7 6 5 4 3 2 1   23 24 25 26 27
Printed in the U.S.A.   40

First printing 2023
Book design by Ashley Vargas

It is raining. Peppa and George have to stay inside.
"I do not like rainy days," Peppa says sadly.

Daddy Pig thinks of a game to play.
He calls it the rainy day game.

He will hide a rubber duck, and George and Peppa will find the duck.

Peppa thinks that the game sounds too easy.

She thinks that George should find the duck first.

Daddy Pig hides the duck in the bedroom.

George cannot find the duck.

"You can see it! Just look with your eyes," says Daddy Pig.

George uses his eyes.
"You are getting warmer,"
Daddy Pig says.

George finds the rubber duck. Peppa still thinks that the game is too easy.

It is Peppa's turn to find the
duck.
Mummy Pig hides the duck in
the kitchen.

Peppa cannot find the duck.
Mummy Pig says, "The duck is
sitting with something that is
yellow."

"Bananas!" says Peppa.
She finds the duck.

The rainy day game is fun!
Peppa wants to play it again.

Daddy Pig puts the duck somewhere for George and Peppa to find together.

Peppa and George cannot find
the duck.

"Where is the duck?" Peppa asks.

Daddy Pig says, "It is sitting on something very big and very wise."

"And very handsome," says Mummy Pig.

The duck is on Daddy Pig's head!

"That is the best hiding place
ever!" Peppa says.

Outside, the rain has stopped.

"I want to play the rainy day game again," says Peppa.

"I can think of an outside rainy
day game that you might like,"
says Daddy Pig.
"What is it?" asks Peppa.

Daddy Pig says, "We need to find a muddy puddle."

"I found it!" Peppa says.
"What do you do when you
find a muddy puddle?" Daddy Pig
asks.

Jump up and down in it!

Peppa likes rainy day games.
Peppa really likes muddy puddles.

Play your own rainy day game, just like Peppa and her family!

1. Have the youngest person in your family pick out a small stuffed animal that they want hidden.

2. The oldest person in your family will hide the stuffed animal somewhere, while everyone else closes their eyes and counts to twenty.

3. When you all open your eyes, it is time to find the stuffed animal! Whoever finds it first gets to hide it next.

4. If you are playing with someone much younger than you, make sure to hide the stuffed animal somewhere they can find it. You can use clues and hints, just like Peppa and her family do.

5. Have fun!